Welcome to Sunny's Salon.

D1502319

Sunny runs the salon with her friends.

Blair is all about organization.
For her, planning means perfection.

Doodle is Sunny's BDFF—
Best Dog Friend Forever!

Put some wild in your style!
Add cool colors to the girls' hair.

Blair is helping Sunny train for a topiary contest.
She gets to cut and style a tree!

Rox wants Sunny to win the contest.
But Lacey wins every year!

Sunny isn't worried.
She shows her plans to her friends.
She's going to cut a tree to look just like Doodle!

"I want everybody to know how great you are,"
Sunny tells Doodle.

Sunny takes her friends to the salon's rooftop garden to show them her tree for the contest.

After Sunny and her friends leave the garden, Lacey and KC land a hot-air balloon on the roof.

They don't want Sunny to enter the contest,
so they take her tree!

Back in the salon, Sunny finishes Timmy's haircut,
then adds a little gel.

Rox is glad Timmy is judging the contest,
because he likes Sunny.
Rox thinks that might help Sunny win.

Sunny wants the contest to be fair.
"I want to *earn* that blue ribbon!"

When Sunny returns to the rooftop garden,
she sees that her tree is gone!

Sunny isn't worried.
She decides to find another tree.

"There has to be a tree in need of a haircut somewhere in Friendly Falls!" says Sunny.

"Ready, set, gear up, and go!"
the friends cry.

While Blair watches the salon, Sunny, Rox, and Doodle race off in the Glam Van.

"First stop—Peter's Flower Shop!"
says Sunny.

Lacey and KC are making their getaway
with the tree on Lacey's moped.

Lacey spots the Glam Van and tells KC to hide Sunny's tree.

At the flower shop, Peter says he has no more trees.
"Everyone bought them for the contest."

"But," Peter adds, "a few of those folks bought *two* trees just in case, so somebody might have an extra. Try Johnny-Ray!"

"We'll look for him," says Sunny.
"Thanks!"

Back in the Glam Van, they see something strange.

A chicken-shaped topiary is crossing the street!
It's Johnny-Ray with his contest entry.

"I love your topiary!" says Rox.
"Do you have an extra tree?"
Johnny-Ray says he only has his chicken tree,
but Cindy might have an extra.

"Next stop—Cindy's Bakery!"
says Sunny.

Cindy messed up her first tree and had to use
her second one—which she gave an interesting look.

Cindy doesn't have an extra tree for Sunny,
but she does have delicious cupcakes for them.

Add some bright colors to these cupcakes.

When Rox throws out the empty cupcake box,
she spots Sunny's missing tree!
The friends wonder who took it.

"We're not far from Lacey and KC's house,"
says Doodle. "Do you think . . . ?"

Meanwhile, Lacey is finishing her spider topiary.

Lacey and KC are on their way to the contest.
They run into Sunny and her friends.

"I thought you'd be home working on your topiary for the contest," Lacey says.

"Don't worry—I'll be at the contest," replies Sunny.
"And I'll have an entry ready to go."

"Face it, Sunny—you're out of time!" Lacey says.
She and KC ride away.

Rox and Doodle think Lacey might be right.
Does Sunny have enough time to style her tree?

Sunny stays positive.
"Time to get to work!" she says.

While Rox drives the Glam Van to the contest, Sunny sets up her haircutting equipment in the back.

Doodle strikes a pose.
"Sunny's really capturing my natural good looks!"

Back at the salon, Blair tells the arriving contestants where to sit.

Lacey is not impressed by the competition.
"Without Sunny in the contest, we're sure to win."

Just then, Sunny arrives with her finished entry.
It looks exactly like Doodle!

"You're not going to get away with being better than me!" shouts Lacey.

Lacey jumps onto a salon chair and uses two
dryers to blow the leaves off Sunny's tree!

Sunny tosses a tube of hair gel toward the chair.

The gel hits a lever, and the chair
spins out of control.

Sunny's topiary is ruined.
"My beautiful head!" cries Doodle.

Just then, Judge Timmy arrives.
"What happened?" he asks.

"Sunny doesn't have an entry,
so I'm obviously the winner," says Lacey.

Sunny has an idea. She asks if the rules say the topiary has to be made from a tree.

Timmy says topiaries don't have to be trees,
so Sunny goes to work on her own hair!

"Ta-da!" says Sunny.
"My official entry: the Doodle Doggie Do!"

Sunny's topi-*hairy* wins first place!

"Who wants a silly old first-prize ribbon anyway?"
says Lacey. She and KC stomp off with their topiary.

Now all Sunny's friends want her to style
their hair like topiaries!

Keep smiling, keep styling . . .
and never give up—even when things get
topi-*hairy*!